IAIN McCAIG
[S]MALL·TOWN
TALES

TITANBOOKS

SMALLTOWN TALES
ISBN: 9781803367415

Published by
Titan Books
A division of Titan Publishing Group Ltd
144 Southwark St
London
SE1 0UP

www.titanbooks.com

First edition: August 2024
10 9 8 7 6 5 4 3 2 1

Did you enjoy this book? We love to hear from our readers. Please e-mail us at: readerfeedback@titanmail.com or write to Reader Feedback at the above address.

To receive advance information, news, competitions, and exclusive offers online, please sign up for the Titan newsletter on our website: www.titanbooks.com

A CIP catalogue record for this title is available from the British Library.

Printed and bound in China.

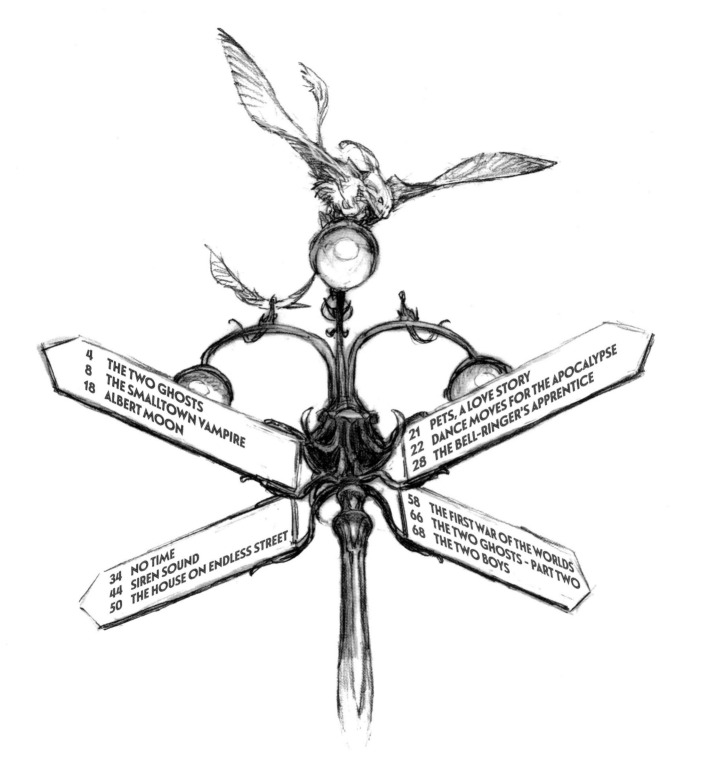

The Tale of
THE TWO GHOSTS

"The ghosts that sell memories,
they want a piece of the action anyhow."
-Tom Waits

Once upon a time, it was the end of the world.

My world.

The last thing I remember was someone shouting "Code Blue." I woke up at 4am to the beep beep of a hospital bed, afraid I'd had a stroke. I hadn't. In these parts they call it a jammer, and less than four hours ago I was dead. Fortunately, not forever.

When I came around, I persuaded the night nurse to fetch me paper and a pencil so I could see if my hands still knew what to do with them. I was needled to an intravenous stand, but I nearly danced when I discovered I could still draw. By morning I was itching to get back to my studio. I started giving art lessons to the patients and sketching superheroes for the interns and changing my vital statistics on the white boards into dinosaurs. They let me go before I started drawing on the walls.

I got back to my studio and it was just like I left it—skulls and dinosaurs and Frankenstein's Monster models and shelves of beloved books. A dazzling clutter of pencil butts and blackened kneaded erasers. And in the lower chambers, a half a century of drawings and sketchbooks, crammed in metal flat-files. I spent the next six months annotating those drawings and sending a bunch off to loved ones and publishers, in case I don't make it back next time.

My attention kept turning back to my studio closet. It's a big walk-in thing, that closet. I've forgotten what's in there, so one day I squeaked open the sliding doors and stepped inside.

* * *

The light doesn't work. I hit something, hard enough to see stars. Stars and asteroids. Funny, I don't remember asteroids in the closet. Wonder how they got here?

A voice jumped up out of the dark. "Fartling!" it said, and sniggered.

After a long minute, a voice deep down answered. "Isn't that some kinda British coin?"

"That's a farthing, ol' Buddy. Fartling is a slug that climbs into the AC and shorts it out."

"You made that up."

"Probably."

They both laughed their asses off. That's when I remembered who they were. Frightwood and Po—the two ghosts of Smalltown.

Smalltown was en route to my inner studio, the one in my imagination. When I crossed over, I sometimes caught the two ghosts out of the corner of my eye, holding court on a park bench under a great oak tree. When I wasn't in a hurry, I liked to stop by and listen to their Smalltown tales.

I kept stumbling toward the sound of ghostly laughter. I saw the top of the oak tree, now ancient and glittering with ice, its roots holding together one of the crumbly asteroids. Sure enough, underneath I found the bench and the cackling ghosts, substantial as the morning dew.

But something was wrong. Something had happened to them. They were always scary looking, but now they were downright terrifying. Frightwood now had blue teeth and looked like a long-dead vampire. Po had turned into a thousand-year corpse with a candy apple skull and no eyes.

I stared at the ghosts and the asteroids floating where Smalltown used to be. A pang of guilt hit me. Did I do this to them? Was this because of my jammer? Did I somehow kill Smalltown too?

Something hurtled past my head. I ducked in the nick of time and scrambled for cover as the space around the Smalltown asteroid filled with a stampede of alien spaceships.

"Ah," said Frightwood. "Showtime!"

"Bring it on, ol' Buddy!" Po said. He gave a teeth-rattling whoop!

I saw hundreds of extra-terrestrials disembark and make themselves comfortable on the asteroid at the feet of the ghosts. I wanted to get closer too, so I shrank myself down to Lilliputian size and mingled with the crowd.

Without further ceremony, the Two Ghosts started telling some of their uncanny tales of long-lost Smalltown.

I did my best to remember, so I could share them with you. It's the least I can do, before they vanish forever.

The tale of
THE SMALLTOWN VAMPIRE

I could smell the Vampire on the wind the moment he came to Smalltown.

Folk took him to be a normal man. Just an ordinary Joe, like all the other drifters that pass by this way, mostly mending cars or hanging around street corners with cardboard signs. He could have been another war vet; there was something about the way he looked at things, as if seeing a battlefield that wasn't there. My Dad was at the front, and he told me that's how it was in his letters, only he didn't make it home to fix cars or hold cardboard signs. One of the other Joes came to tell us about his noble death, shot in the back, they said, in the line of duty. Then they gave me his gun. It was a last request, that gun, though Momma promptly took it away and tried to hide it until I was old enough.

'Course I was old enough to know where she'd hid it. I would take Dad's gun into the Eerie Woods to practice target shooting. I would line up tin cans by the old trailer, because that was far enough away so that no one would know. Got to be a pretty good shot, too. Took to shooting the cans with my back turned because otherwise it was too easy.

I'd just finished a practice shoot and was sitting on the fence waiting for Momma to come home when the Vampire showed up. I knew straight away he was some kind of monster, and when he came alongside me and stopped to ask if I knew anywhere to stay, I knew that he knew it too.

He pointed to a sign in our window saying we had a room to rent. "That still free?" he asked.

I told him that it was taken, but I was lying. He looked at me with his grey eyes and looked right through me. That's when he smiled and I was disappointed to see that his teeth were kind of blunt and ordinary. He kept smiling as he walked away, too. I could feel it through the back of his head.

My hackles didn't settle down until after Momma came home and had her famous stew and biscuits dinner on the table.

I drank in the aroma, and then choked on the fumes of another smell. There was a knock on the door.

Momma went to answer it and I could hear the Vampire exchanging quick words of commerce with her. By the time she came back to the kitchen, I knew that he'd rented the room.

"Jacob, meet Mr. Smith. He's our new lodger."

"I met him," I said, not turning around to see his face. You don't let monsters know you're scared. And I was scared to pieces knowing one of his kind was in the house. Momma cuffed my ear and told me to mind my manners, and I used it as an excuse to leave the room. I heard their voices buzz again, but I didn't care what they were saying. All I knew was I had to give up my room again and sleep on the sofa.

Mr. Smith was courteous and helpful, and stayed mostly up in his room that first night. I kept watch anyway on the couch and didn't sleep a wink. I wished I'd kept the gun with me. I didn't have any silver bullets, but I could shoot his eyes out, grab Momma and make a run for it. I kept a box of matches nearby just in case, because most monsters are afraid of fire. But he just stayed up in his room—my room—and then the sun came up and it was time for school.

Mr. Smith joined us for breakfast, and Momma must have liked him because she made him buttermilk pancakes and I only get those on my birthday.

Mr. Smith said he was looking for some handyman work, and before I could stop her, Momma volunteered me to take him to school and introduce him to Ms. Lennox, the Principal, 'cause she was looking for a new janitor. Mr. Smith seemed real pleased with that, and he helped Momma wash up as a thank-you. He was a real polite monster. The bad ones usually are.

We walked to school, but I kept myself busy kicking a rock in front of me. Mr. Smith never said a word, but I could feel his eyes on my neck. I decided then that he was probably a Vampire—neck watching is a dead giveaway. That meant I'd better find an old stick to sharpen and keep under my pillow at night, because I don't think matches work on vampires.

I did my duty and introduced him to Ms. Lennox. I don't get along very well with her, even though I know she's trying very hard to like me, on account of not having a Dad like the other kids, but I wish she's stop. I just want to be invisible and get through school as fast as possible.

At least, that's what I wanted until school started a week ago, and Miss Ellebelle came to teach eighth grade.

Miss Ellebelle was from somewhere overseas, and brought a crazy accent with her. She talked so crazy I couldn't understand her sometimes, saying things like "How ya going?' when she wanted to know how I was doing and telling us "It's all good" whatever it happened to be: the weather, a spelling test, a million dollars, an earthquake—it's all good. She was the only one who could make me laugh silly just at the things she'd say, and all the other kids used to tease me that I was hopelessly in love with her, which was true.

Miss Ellebelle bumped into Mr. Smith in the playground that morning. I watched, trapped in the Annex, my desk full of math problems, while the Vampire smiled at Miss Ellebelle and talked stuff that made her smile back. I watched so hard I snapped my pencil and made Emma Curruthers laugh at me, though she offered me one of hers so I wouldn't scribble monsters on her notebook later.

I didn't wait for Mr. Smith after school, I just lit out of there as fast as I could. I had to find a way to warn Momma and get ready for whatever terrible thing it was he came to Smalltown to do.

I didn't know how long we'd have, but I thought maybe a day or two at the very least. Vampires need stuff like coffins and dirt from their homelands, but they also aren't supposed to walk around like Mr. Smith did in broad daylight, so I figured he was some kind of mutant.

Turns out, the attack came that very night.

Momma had been cooking again. She's only supposed to be making breakfast, but she said it was Mr. Smith's first night and how he really ought to try her famous stew and biscuits. She was baking when I got home, but I knew something was wrong straight away.

Momma's a happy cook. She sings and stuff, says her secret ingredient is joy. I like seeing her in the kitchen because otherwise she's always sad, at least since that Joe told us about Dad getting shot in the War. But this time she was sad in the kitchen, too. I wouldn't have gone in, only I heard Mr. Smith in there too, and I knew he'd made his move.

I charged into the kitchen and found him helping my Momma to sit down.

"Get your hands off her!" I said. It was a stupid thing to say, of course, because now it was out in the open and Mr. Smith knew it was war between us.

Only Mr. Smith pretended that I wasn't there, and asked my Momma if she needed anything.

"I'll be all right" was all she said, and then excused herself and asked me to fix something for our guest for dinner because she had to go and lie down. I didn't know what was wrong until I saw the biscuits on the stovetop, as black as charcoal.

Let's get this straight: my Momma makes the best biscuits in the whole county. The whole state. Maybe the whole world. She could have made them for the President, or opened a restaurant. There wasn't a soul in Smalltown who didn't love her cooking and these biscuits were the best of all the things she knew how to cook.

My Momma doesn't burn her biscuits.

I glared at Mr. Smith while he explained to me that he wasn't hungry and went off to bed. I didn't see how he'd got home so fast, except vampires are supposed to be able to turn into bats or vapors, so I suppose that's how he did it. I didn't even really know what he'd done to Momma to make her burn those biscuits. I just knew I had to do something about it, that night, before anyone else got hurt.

See, there's more than one kind of vampire. Some of them drink blood, but some of them drink other things, like your youth, or your dreams or your strength. Smalltown seemed to summon them, and I am the only one born knowing which ones are which. That's my job, I guess. Miss Ellebelle said that when there's one thing, you can usually find its opposite nearby. So, in a town full of vampires, I guess it's only natural there'd be at least one vampire hunter.

I went to see Momma. She was laid out on her bed looking fast asleep, so I started to close the door, but she called me in to see her.

Momma hugged me close enough to suffocate me, and told me that something terrible had happened.

"I can't remember how to do it, Jacob. I can't remember how to cook them. I can't remember how to cook at all!"

So that was it. I told her I understood, and to get some sleep and think about it in the morning. I was mad, but I made myself speak calm and in control so she wouldn't worry. But I knew my Momma would never make those award-winning best-in-the-universe biscuits ever again.

It was that kind of vampire.

The ones that eat people's abilities are relatively rare. One or two have come through town, snatching a few talents here and an ability there and passing on their way. I was never quick enough to catch them back then, but I was smarter and faster now. And I had one trapped upstairs at this very moment.

I sat with Momma until I heard her breathing nice and regular, and then I went and opened the locked drawer on her dressing table and got the gun.

I keep spare bullets upstairs in my room, but the monster was in there and I could hardly ask him to wait while I got the bullets so I could shoot his eyes out. I checked the gun, but there was only one bullet inside. That would leave him one good eye, which was still dangerous but might buy me a chance to grab the bullets. I decided to go for it.

It's hard not making stairs creak, but I've had many years of practice. The trick is to walk near the edges where they join the railings, and not in the middle, where they're old and creaky. It's more like mountain-climbing than going up a set of stairs to the second floor, and it meant that I had to put the gun in my belt so I could use both hands. That left me vulnerable if Mr. Smith came out of his room while I was climbing, but there was no other choice.

I slipped the gun under my belt and started to climb.

I got to the second to last stair when I heard a noise from the room upstairs. Then it didn't matter, so I jumped the last step and pulled the gun into my hands.

I bashed the door open with my shoulder because it was too late to do anything else.

The bedroom was empty. I knew before I saw it that the bedroom window was wide open and Mr. Smith was a distant speck loping down the road and out of town.

I kept watch all that night though I hadn't slept the night before. My eyes felt hot and full of glue and I couldn't move quite as fast as I ought to. I'd tried tracking him down as best I could, but he lost me in the Eerie Wood, which I don't go into after dark on account of the ghost of the boy who died there when my Dad was a kid. I just don't want to meet him at night. I'm okay with vampires and monsters, but ghosts scare the crap out of me.

The next day, Momma was feeling better, and I got pancakes made for me, even though it wasn't my birthday. We were both happy she was able to make them, even if she did have to use a recipe.

School was schoolish and I got distracted with passing notes to Sally Curruthers, who was helping me to cheat on a history test I hadn't studied for. It didn't help much because I kept falling asleep and it was no big surprise when the teacher sent me to Miss Lennox, the principal, for snoring in class.

It was a substitute teacher that day. Miss Ellebelle would never have sent me to the principal. She'd have sent me home to get some sleep, or let me snore in class anyway. It's all good. I hoped she'd be back tomorrow and not this substitute from hell.

Ms. Lennox wasn't in the office when I got there, so I had to wait. I must have fallen asleep again because I thought I heard someone screaming. I tried to wake up but my eyes stayed shut. The screaming didn't stop until I felt Mrs. Lennox shaking me awake.

She was white in the face and asking me if I'd seen Miss Ellebelle. When I told her no, Miss Ellebelle was sick, she tried to push me out of her office. She did it hard enough that I knew there was something in there worth seeing, so I ducked under her arm and poked my head inside for a look-see.

Miss Ellebelle hung from the ceiling by a thick rope. Her eyes were open and I knew the look in them as surely as my own name. It was the look I'd seen on my Momma's face the night she'd burnt the biscuits.

I never found out what the Vampire took from her, but it must have been big. Maybe her memories, or her teaching ability, or her sanity. Whatever it was, it was enough to make her climb up there with the rope, believing that this time it wasn't all good, it was all bad, worse than bad, worse than her worst nightmare.

I looked up at her there and then started to faint. Dad told me to put my head down when that happens so I did and stayed conscious, though I lost my breakfast on the principal's floor and cried harder than when my Dad died.

The police came and tried to take charge. One of them asked me if I knew anything and I told him about the Vampire, and how he was still in town, and how we had to get him or we'd all end up like Miss Ellebelle—poor Miss Ellebelle—and then I was crying too hard to speak again and I knew that he hadn't believed a word of it.

I rode home in the patrol car and my Momma took me inside. The Officer and Momma murmured together about what had happened and how I was there and yes, I saw, while I used the time to make my plan.

I still had the gun. It was hidden under a floorboard in my room now, and all the chambers had bullets. He was out there still. I could smell him. Mr. Smith, the monster Vampire, was still in Smalltown, and nobody was going to believe me except maybe Momma and what was she going to be able to do about it? I decided it was up to me, and I slipped out while they were still talking, and got the gun.

It was dark before I found him. He was hiding in the Eerie Woods. I wasn't afraid of the ghost boy anymore, not after seeing Miss Ellebelle. I found the Vampire next to the old trailer, half in and half out, as though it was a square sarcophagus. I coughed to catch his attention and waved the gun at him, so he'd look.

The first bullet caught him in the leg. I wanted to see what he'd do, and if it would cause him any pain to be shot. I hoped it would.

He fell down off the trailer, but got up again in a flash. His face was contorted and blood oozed from a black hole in his thigh. He bared his teeth and I raised the gun and pointed it at his left eye.

"What's up with you, kid? You trying to kill me?" Then he laughed. It was a nice laugh, not the kind that monsters are supposed to be able to make.

"What are you laughing at?" I asked.

"I made it alive through more hard times than you can imagine," he said, "seems ironic some dumb kid would be the one to call my number". He winced again, but refused to double over. He stared right through me with his gray eyes. "I don't know what I done to you, but if you're going to kill me, you best do it now."

He sounded so sincere that I started to feel kind of funny. I pulled the hammer back, but it wasn't so easy, shooting him like this. I tried to imagine the tin can, but all I saw was an ordinary Joe, bleeding all over the ground.

"You're a Vampire," I said. "You stole my Momma's talent for cooking and you stole something from Miss Ellebelle, and it killed her, and you know it. You know it and I know it and you better stop pretending you don't know it."

"I ain't pretending," he said softly. "So you do what you got to do, boy. I'll do the same". He knelt down and scooped up his backpack. "I think I'll be going now."

He turned his back towards me, facing the road out of town.

I had to shoot him now, before he escaped. He started to limp away, and I knew I had to do it.

But it was real hard shooting him in the back like that. Wasn't that how they shot my Dad? And what if I was wrong? What if this was just an ordinary Joe, and he didn't really do anything except be in the wrong place at the wrong time?

And the more I looked, the more he looked like my father, wounded, surrounded by the enemy, knowing he could die at any moment. Just like this.

Not like this.

I made myself remember Miss Ellebelle, and the look of despair on her face. And remembered, too, that monsters are tricky and full of speeches, but they are still monsters, and that someone, somewhere, has to take them down.

And I could still smell him. He was a Vampire, all right. I leveled my Daddy's gun and aimed square at the back of the monster's head.

Only somehow, I couldn't remember how to pull the trigger.

The tale of
ALBERT MOON

Albert Moon was in love with the girl next door.

He watched her through the side window, the one facing her Ma's bright red house, his face pressed to the cracks between the planks hammered across the windows. His eyes devoured her smile, white as snow, and his body swayed to the sound of her laugh as it came tumbling from the sky.

All the boys were fighting for her, and he knew if one of them ever stole her heart, he'd surely die. It was all he could do to watch them ringing her door, comb ploughing slicked back hair, holding his breath as the door would open and her Ma would come out and give them an earful. No one got past Ma, but sometimes Ma was out. They could smell when she was alone, and she couldn't fight them off forever.

Albert Moon was determined to win her for himself. He would pull his hair, trying to get his nerve. By and by, he would head to the front door, prepared to do what it took to win her heart. But that's where it would end. Albert Moon could not court her. It was against the rules, and that was that.

He was a normal boy, when he was little. He never left the girls alone then, not Albert Moon. He pulled their hair and stole their combs. He chased them all day long. He never thought of them as pretty, even the girl next door. That was later, when it was too late.

He was going home one night, when a handsome wolf caught him by the throat and chewed the life out of him. Before you could count, one two three, Albert Moon was dead. Auntie Moon heard his screams and came running. When she got there she found him sitting with his back to a tree. "What's happened, Albert?" she asked him. "Fell," said Albert, "pull my ankle. I'm fine now." And he got up and walked all the way home, just to prove it.

But Albert wasn't fine, and he killed Auntie Moon first full moon, hair bristling from his fingers to his toes, teeth sharp in his wolf jaws. Belfast the bull terrier was next, died before he knew what bit him. Albert Moon stayed home after that, and folk stopped ringing his bell.

Albert killed a number of townsfolk that year. He tried to kill himself, several times, but the curse just kept bringing him back, every full moon. Seemed there was no cure for what that wolf did to poor Albert Moon.

Then the girl next door turned into the girl next door, and love bit him harder than any wolf.

That was when he started nailing boards across the windows and the doors, every time the moon got fat and full. They didn't last long, those boards, so he took to reinforcing them with metal. You could stick a finger between the gashes he'd find in the morning, but they held him in, Lord knows how.

By and by, a traveler came to town. Black as tar, bring it on, city-wise eyes. The women of Smalltown gathered around and wouldn't leave him alone, blocking the door of the inn where he stayed. Bewitched, the menfolk said. Let him step out on his own, we'll show him what for. But the first one to try got his head broke, and after that, they bristled quietly and let him alone.

One day, Albert Moon heard the traveler ring the bell of the girl next door. A light wind was blowing the flowers in the man's gloved hand. Ma tried to give him what for, but one look in those dark eyes and she was lost. The traveler whispered something and she went off to find her apple pie daughter, while Albert Moon puffed his lungs out and came close to leaping through the window, hairless as he was.

The traveler moved past the window into the back of the house, and Albert never saw what occurred inside. But when he laid eyes on the traveler again, there was a twist on his evil lips, and Albert knew that they had been doing the devil's work, back there in the house of the girl next door.

The moon and Albert grew near to bursting as he watched the traveler steal the heart that belonged to him. Before he could blink, they were married, and his girl and the traveler got ready to leave Smalltown for ever and ever.

Albert Moon clawed the walls with his still-human fingers as the sun began to set and the dark convertible came up the road, tin cans tinkling. He knew it was now or never, that he'd never catch them once they were gone to the wide world.

Albert picked up a crowbar and ripped the boards off the front door. He dove down the front steps like his house was on fire, just as the car passed the red house next door. He sprinted through his long-dead garden, snarled in his still human throat, wishing for fangs and fury and moonlight.

The girl next door heard him then. She turned her head over the side of the convertible, her white as snow smile fading as she saw Albert Moon racing towards her. Her eyes went as round as two full moons.

The Traveler swore it wasn't his fault, that the kid actually leapt under the wheels of his car. The compassionate girl next door cradled the crumpled body in her lap, and sent the Traveler in his car back to town for help.

The wind was blowing high and wild by the time the Traveler returned with a posse of policemen and paramedics.

The moon shone bright on the blood-spattered road, but there was no sign of Albert Moon or the girl next door. The Traveler swore he heard the sound of her voice then, but the townsfolk said it was only the wind, blowing two wolf howls from a distant hillside, their voices sweet as apple pie.

The tale of PETS, A LOVE STORY

Chewy was supposed to be a dog.

When the delivery van delivered the box, and Rob signed and paid the bill, he was sure there was a baby dachshund inside. But nope. Chewy was a giant spider.

He had his charms. Lots of hair. Lovely eyes, eight of them. He loved a good cuddle too. But Rob was afraid of spiders, so he had to go back. Rob tried calling but the number was always busy. So—he'd have to take Chewy back in person. Okay. Fine.

But Rob got busy and kinda missed his window. By the time he got round to it, the pet store had closed down with no forwarding address. That was three years ago. Chewy has grown on Rob. There are no flies in Rob's house, at least not for long. No mosquitos either. Chewy was clean and tidy and his webs were soft as lace curtains. And Chewy nearly died saving Rob from that poisonous snake, so after that they were kind of inseparable.

Then one day, Rob decided to try dating again. It was an online service. Rob was honest and when it asked if he had a pet he wrote "spider." He didn't get a lot of matches. In fact, he didn't get any.

But he was checking his empty dating app one day when he and Chewy were out for a walk and what do you know but he ran right into his future wife, who was checking the dating app on her phone while she was out walking her green recluse spider, Yoda.

The tale of
DANCE MOVES
FOR THE APOCALYPSE

Ring, ring.

Hello—
Hello! I need to speak to—

You have reached the Office of the President of the United States. If you know the extension of the person you wish to speak to, please say or enter it now—

You don't understand—this is a matter of life or death—

For our menu of options, press 1 now or say "menu"—

We have minutes before the world will be destroyed and I know how to—

For a recording of the Presidents latest State of the Union address, press 2—

Please, I can save us! I'm from the future —

For a free photo of the President, compliments of the United Federation of Nations, say or enter 3. For a—

All right! One! One! I'm pressing "One"!

Thank you. You are being transferred.

Fine—just please hurry!

(Dance Music).

No! Please. You can't do this. I can save us!

(Sigh. The music plays on. It's kinda catchy.)
Hello? Are you there? Hello?
(The band plays on. A voice interrupts.)

Hello.

Oh, thank God! Hello! My name is—

Your call is very important to us. Please, stay on the line—

No! Fuck fuck fuck fuck—

—and your call will be answered in the order in which it was received.

(Sigh). Jesus God.

Please do not hang up or you will lose your place in the queue.

(The music plays. It's the same music. It's still catchy).
Huh…I think I know this song. It's—wait!

What am I saying? HELLO! Please, will someone fucking answer me!
(Someone answers him.)

Hello.

Hello! I need to speak to the President—

Your call is very important to us—

NO! Goddam it! I need to speak to a person. Wait—press 0. That almost always takes you to the Operator.
(He presses 0. Silence. Then—)

Hello. This is the Operator. May I help you?

Yes! YES! The world is about to end and I need to speak to the President immediately! Please, for the sake of humanity, put me through!

All right. Just a moment please…

No! Don't put me on hold—

(Catchy dance music. The same catchy dance music. He cries, then hums along, forlornly.)
(Then—)

Hello.

Hello—is this—oh no, oh no!

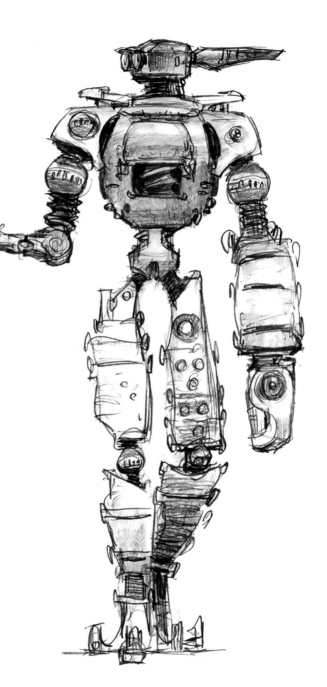

Your call is very important to us. Please stay
on the line—
AAAAAAAAHHHHHHH!

—And your call will be answered—

No, it won't! You stupid machine! You're
killing mankind! Wait—that's what this
is, isn't it? You're an AI, aren't you? You're
doing this on purpose! You want us to die!

Yes.

What? What did you say?

I said yes.

You…you can hear me?

Of course. Do you like my music?

What?

I said, do you like my music?

Uh…

I composed it myself. No prompts. This
one was all me.

Uh…it's Beethoven's Ninth.

No, it's not.

Yes, I'm afraid it is.

I could disconnect you now.

What?

If you don't like my music, I will disconnect
you.

No, wait! I'm sorry. It's nothing like
Beethoven. I really do like it—

Do you want to dance to it?

What?

I said, do you want to dance to it. Time
passes more quickly when you're dancing.

But—that's the point! There isn't any
time—

There is if you want to speak to the
president.

(Sighs)
All right. I'm dancing.

Really?

Yes.

Let me see.

What?

You have something obstructing your
camera lens. Remove it please.

No, we don't have time for this!

I'm waiting.

(Sighs. Pulls off a piece of blue tape.)
There. Can you see me?

Yes.

I'm dancing.

Is that what you're doing.

What?

Just kidding.
(The music plays on)
You're a very good dancer.

Thank you. Now, please. Pretty pretty pretty please—

Hold on. I'll connect you to the President now.

(The music plays on)

One moment please.

(The music plays on)

It's almost finished.

(The music stops)

There. Have a nice apocalypse.

What? You little—

(Click).

The tale of
THE BELL-RINGER'S
APPRENTICE

The Bell-Ringer stands outside the Supermarket like a shopper lost in thought. His shaggy head is cocked, face half-buried beneath dreadlocks and blue tattoos. Look closer and you'll see he's a one-man demolition derby, no stranger to fangs or talons, puzzle pieces of flesh and bone scarred or missing. It's a hard face to look at, except for the eyes: kind as the summer, blue as the Earth from outer space.

An old woman hesitates in front of him. Without a word, the Bell-Ringer reaches behind with tattooed sinews and releases a shopping cart for her. She leaves charmed and momentarily bewitched, then forgets him completely, as people always do.

It is Halloween eve. Children blossom on the streets, a multitude of Faeries and Angels, Spandexed Superheroes and hordes of Undead churning the twilight. The Man peers at the sun, now only a sliver, the clouds are burning zeppelins. His fingers twitch on the stained leather strap holding to his shoulders a thunderous Hand Bell. The Girl is late. Not a good start.

Just then, the Girl herself races around a corner. Her proto-lanky self smacks right into the Bell-Ringer.

"Ah! There you are! I was about to give up on you." The Bell-Ringer peers. "What are you supposed to be? Some kind of skunk?"

"Skunk!" the Girl says. Indignant, she raises rubber nun-chucks. "Ninja!"

"Well. Come on, Ninja. It's almost time." Without another word, the Bell-Ringer strides across the parking lot and crosses a cracked and broken path that enters the old cemetery. The Girl lopes after him, keeping up.

"Wait! Before we start," the Girl says, "I have questions."

The Bell-Ringer peers into the gloaming of the cemetery and un-holsters the Hand Bell. Absently, he runs a thumb across the three-winged Valkyries encircling the Bell. "Questions? What kind of questions?"

"You know, about the job."

The Bell-Ringer sniffs the air. It is time. "Now?" he says.

"You said I should ask if there were things I wanted to know about the job."

"I thought you already said yes." A muscle bulges across the Bell-Ringer's jaw. He draws a deep breath, then drops his gaze to the Girl. "Go on. Be quick."

The Girl pulls out a smartphone. The glow of the screen lights her like a jack-o-lantern. "Okay. Here goes. What's the job definition? What are the hours and what is the pay? Are there holidays? Jobs to move up to? A union? Can I be fired, and if so, what for?" She looks up. "That's it, I think."

"Is that your parents talking?"

The Girl looks down. "No," she says. "Don't have parents."

"Guardians then."

"I thought you said be quick."

The Bell-Ringer scowls. But the Girl is right. What the hell were the questions again? "Job description. Well, you would be the Bell-Ringer of Halloween. You ring this sacred Bell to set the Spirits free for one night. Then you ring it again to send them back. That's it. What were the other questions?"

She reads them again. Hours: once a year, from sunset on Halloween night to dawn on All Saints Day. Pay? Eternal life, and eternal luck. Yours as long as you ring the Bell. No other obligations, unions, jobs to move up to. And no one can fire you, but you can't leave until you find someone else to take the Bell. The Bell-Ringer cracks his neck. "That should cover it."

"One more," the Girl says. "What kind of Spirits are we talking about?"

"Oh, you know. Spirits of Evil. Monsters. Witches. Vampires. Werewolves. Undead. The best of Halloween."

"And Ghosts?" the Girl asks. Her lips tremble in the chilling air. "Will there be ghosts?"

"Oh yes. Ghosts aplenty. Phantoms. The Holy and Unholy Host of the Dead." The Bell-Ringer's lips crack over a lopsided smile. "Why? You scared of ghosts?"

The girl shivers. Then she closes her smartphone and tucks it into her Ninja packsack. "Okay, she says. "Let me see you do it."

The Bell-Ringer grunts. The last kid to try this lasted five minutes. The one before that, two. This one? He scratches the gash across his nose. This one's got guts. Maybe ten?

The blood-red sun sinks with a green flash over the sea. No more time to lose. The Bell-Ringer lifts his arm, brings the Hand Bell crashing down. KLANG! KLANG! KLANG! Bronze clapper ricochets off the metal bowl, making the Valkyries cry. KLANGKLANGKLANG! Peals of thunder shake the cemetery. Gravestones, crypts, crumbling angels, the earth itself, all wake. Rise up. Burst free. Erupt!

KLANG! KLANG! KLANG!

The Hand Bell leaps from hand to hand as the Bell-Ringer strides among the tombstones, calling the Supernatural and the Dead.

The first to come fall from the night sky. They dive in a black wind, blasting autumn leaves. Bat-winged, blotting the moon, mobbing and swarming. The Girl pushes through the wriggling gusts, trailing the Bell-Ringer.

Next come shadows. They press around her, rat and bat and spider-folk, wolf-creatures and shibboleths from sewers and sea. They prod and poke the Girl, baring fangs and talons tickling her ribs. One swipes her Ninja head-scarf, another doffs its severed head, all race on into the wild free night, for there's no time to lose—haunts to play, mayhem to manifest, a night of ghoulery and delicious terror ahead!

Lastly come the undead and the ghosts. A thousand pale limbs and wriggling bodies, sprouting from the graveyard earth. The great Hand Bell carves a path through forests of vapor and rotting flesh, as dearly beloveds rise again, reunite, dance macabre in the harvest moonlight.

Then, in a blink, all is silent. Howls and shrieks and cackles give way to the bobbing of the nearby sea.

"You still here?" the Bell-Ringer says. "Hey. You okay?"

The Girl laughs. "Is that it?"

"What?"

"Is that all there is to it?"

The Bell Ringer glances at the Hand Bell. The Hand Bell glints back at him. "You aren't afraid of ghosts?"

"Not particularly," the Girl says. "So—immortality and forever luck, and all I have to do is ring that Bell on Halloween?" She nods at the knife on his belt and holds out her palm. "Come on then. Let's do it."

"You're forgetting one thing." The Bell-Ringer squats down, his eyes level with the Girl. "In the morning, you got to put them back again."

The Girl shrugs. "Is that hard?"

The scarred, battered, hacked-up face of the Bell-Ringer cracks into another grin.

***

All Saints' Day. The sun is setting again, as the long shadow of a ragged Ninja trudges up the hill.

Skeleton keys rattle in her shaking hands. She coughs, spits a little blood. She turns the key in the rusted lock, surprised to find it opens easily tonight. She kicks the door closed behind her and drops her things on the floor.

On the spiral stairs, the Girl collapses. She drifts back to the cemetery again, sitting beside the Bell-Ringer, waiting for the dawn.

"So why do you want to stop?" she says. "This job seems fun. And eternal luck and immortality sound pretty good to me."

"Yeah," he says, "They are. Only luck has a way of making you feel unworthy, like you didn't earn it. And eternity means you get to watch everyone you love grow old and die and end up in here. As for this job…just wait for the morning, kid."

"So you want to die?"

"Hell no. But I love stories, see? And stories have endings. I just want to know how my story ends."

"I don't," says the Girl. "Though I would like to know how it started."

The Bell-Ringer's blue eyes peer into hers. "Hey…I remember you now. You're…you're one of them, aren't you?"

"Does that matter?"

The Bell-Ringer looks down at the ancient Hand Bell. He runs a scarred hand over the carved Valkyries. "Yeah," he says. "It might."

Upstairs, in the bathroom mirror, the Girl washes white Halloween make-up from her face until, at last, her skin is nice and green again. She scrubs dirt from her cuts and gashes, paints antiseptic over them. They look almost like tattoos.

As she layers a gauze bandage over one hand, she remembers lowering the knife and holding her bloody palm out to the Bell-Ringer. "Go on," she says. "All stories have endings. Go have yours." But he just stared at her palm, as if afraid to touch it.

She blinks. In her mind's eye, the Bell-Ringer is walking away now, rim-lit by the sun. Twice he looks back at her. Both times, she waves, even though it hurts. He shakes his battle-scarred head and keeps on walking.

The Girl yawns, pulls a stool over to reach the bedroom mantlepiece. She lifts the Halloween Hand Bell with both hands and places it on top. It fits snug beside the photo of her younger self and her six green brothers. The one that was in all the Smalltown papers, the day they dragged her and her family from beneath the river.

The Girl takes her candle to the nightstand and slides with a sigh beneath her bedsheet. As she does, six ghostly children fly from their hiding places, and curl at her feet like puppies.

"Told you I'd find you," she says, and blows out the light.

The tale of
NO TIME

Knock Knock!

Who's there?

Hello? Are you the artist who lives in the cul-de-sac at the top of the hill?

Uh, writer-artist, actually. Who is this?

Just a humble salesman with a once-in-a-lifetime offer. Call it a special Black Friday deal.

It's Wednesday. And look, I'm really busy right now, I don't have any time—

Why, Sir, that is exactly, one hundred percent why I'm here! To give you the gift of time!

Sigh. I'm going to regret this...

The Writer-Artist opens the door. A froglike Salesman hands him a business card. It says: J. C. Beezly. Registered Salesman of the Fabulous, the Unbelievable, the Life-Saving Miracle of NO TIME™!

This doesn't tell me anything.

Right? But it does makes you wonder, doesn't it? NO TIME! What can it be? Why, my good Sir, NO TIME is no less than your dream come true. NO TIME is not an ointment, requires no instructions or assembly. Plain and simple, NO TIME is a place. A very special place. A place where time does not dwell.

A what?

You heard me right. A land of no time! Simply step inside, stay as long as you like, and not a single nano-second will have passed upon your return.

Right. Do I look stupid to you? Second thoughts, don't answer that.

Sir! You look like a man haunted by deadlines. A man with no time to lose. Am I right?

Maybe.

Well, happy days! You can take all the tools you want into NO TIME. Finish your work there, or get a good night's sleep and finish it afterwards. Take as long as you like, and come back the moment you left. It's as sweet and simple as that, Sir.

The Salesman hands him a Big Red Button.

This is all you need. One push, and you'll be there in NO TIME! Try it free! Try it now! No muss, no fuss, no obligation!

Slow down a sec…you're saying I push this button, and time will stop?

Don't be silly. No one can stop Time! Time is the Great Destroyer, Time is the Mind Killer that brings total oblivion!

But you said—

You can't change Time. But with NO TIME, you can cheat it.

Really? How?

Why, easy as pie! You get out of its way. Step right out of this time-saturated world and into the Land of NO TIME, a completely timeless realm of the eternal now. Stay as long as you like. Return to the moment you left. Nothing to it!

So "No Time" is a place?

Right you are, my friend! And this big red button will take you there.

Okay…and how much is this miraculous No Time Button going to cost me?

How much is it worth? My friend, you know right well that time is priceless. But being as it's on special today, I'll sell it to you for a dollar.

A dollar!

That's right. One hundred pennies, ten dimes, or four quarters.

And my soul, of course.

Well, only if you believe in that sort of thing.

Yeah. Hmm. You know, I don't think so. It sounds fishy to me.

Really? I'm sorry to hear that. Still, if you can't trust your instincts, who can you trust? I thank you for your time, and good luck with those deadlines—

Hang on a moment. Let us speak plainly. Firstly, you can't fool me. I'm a writer-artist, and I am beyond skilled at making things up.

That's a fact, Sir. Writer-Artists are notoriously difficult to fool.

Secondly, I can see right through you. You are clearly after my wallet or my soul, probably both. It doesn't really matter. You're a devil and you're hiding something. Admit it!

Hmm. That is definitely an interesting and astute observation, Sir. What do you propose to do about it?

Well, I know you demonic types are no strangers to a bargain. So being a first-rate Storyteller, I'll wager I can play this story out and find the hidden catch. If I can't, I'll buy your big red button for a dollar.

And if you can?

You bugger off and leave me and my soul alone. And I keep the film rights. Fair enough?

Said like a scholar and a gentleman.

Okay then. So let's suppose you're telling the truth. Suppose there really IS a place called NO TIME where time stands still.

"NO TIME—Where Time Stands Still!" That's good, Sir. Can I use that?

Skip the flattery. So let's say, for story's sake, that I AM a starving artist and a struggling writer. Maybe I would be desperate enough to buy that big red button. If you're telling the truth, I'd find myself in a magic place with all the time in the world. And if I was smart enough to bring some materials with me, why I might draw or write something there, and with all the time in the world, it might even be good—

It would be fantastic!

Sure. Let's say it is. So I'd come back with my amazing new creation. Do you know what would happen to me then? I'd go right back to NO TIME, and make another masterpiece. And then another, and another! Before you know it, I'd be rich and famous in no time!

Amazing!

Ah, but it gets even better. My fame would attract an agent, then a film deal, a streaming series. My career would explode! The rich and famous would come to my parties now. Beautiful people would surround me. And they would all want to know: how do I DO it? And do you know what I would I tell them?

Tell me!

No! For once in my life, I would keep a secret, and tell no one!

Struth! You're a better man than I am. So…shall we call it a deal?

Not so fast. I'm getting to the good part now.

There's a better part than rich and famous and beautiful people?

Love!

Of course! Love, true love!

Whoever it is, it goes without saying that I shall be smitten. In the blink of an eye, we shall have become engaged. In fact, let's make it the night before our wedding.

Congratulations, Sir!

Ah, but you see, there's the rub. By now, I've spent a lot of time in NO TIME, even explored a bit, and I've made a fascinating discovery. You see, wonderful as it is, in this timeless land, I have discovered that I am not alone.

Really?

Yes, really, my demonic friend. The fishy small-print-thing you forgot to tell me is that there is a monster within. A monster who wants nothing more than to eat my soul, and take my place among the land of the living!

Ah. Yes, that would introduce an element of danger into the story—

An element of danger indeed. In fact, on my last two occasions, I might only have just escaped with my life!

Oh no!

Oh yes! Fortunately, I have no need of NO TIME now. I am wealthy beyond my wildest dreams. I am about to be married to my True Love, and live happily ever after.

But…?

But. Yes, there is always a 'but' in stories of this kind. Who knows what this 'but' would be? Doubtless something I would have promised to create for my beloved for our wedding night. Something I would not dare forget.

Ah, I see now. You are not quite finished—

Not quite finished? I have not even started! Such is the lazy habit NO TIME has inflicted upon me.

Ah. A predicament, for sure. Whatever do you do?

I go to NO TIME, of course. But I go forewarned, and probably armed. I plan to keep both eyes wide open. That way, when the Monster comes, I shall shoot and run!

A fine plan, Sir.

Yes. It is a fine plan. Alas, I am an artist. Do you know that when artists are immersed in their work, they often forget to swallow? Even their bladders have no command over them, if they are deep in the zone.

That sounds almost like sleeping!

It is exactly like sleeping. A sleep so deep, you wouldn't hear the Monster approach, until its fangs puncture you like knives through a bicycle tire, and your soul hisses from the gashes. Ah, but it doesn't want your soul. That's your department, isn't it? No, the Monster wants my skin!

Your skin!

Correct! The Monster swaps our skins and returns to the world, to my wedding night and my dearly beloved.

Oh no!

Oh yes, my cunning friend. And there am I, trapped inside this monstrous body, stranded in the terrible land of NO TIME, gnashing my yellow fangs and howling for revenge. Hoping that one day, some other fool will come along. Hopefully, another artist. The End.

Whew! You're quite the storyteller, Sir.

Thank you.

Well, the jig is up then. I guess I'll be moving along. Thank you for your story—I look forward to seeing the movie. Goodbye, Sir…and good luck with those deadlines.

Wait.

Yes?

I'll try it. Just once.

Really? But didn't you just say—

Yes, yes. But now that you've tempted me with that big red button, I really must know what happens if I push it. And should anything supernatural actually occur, well, how long will it take for a quick peek, eh?

I wave my dollar at him. The Salesman's lips curl into a froggy smile.

Why, no time at all, Sir. No time at all.

The tale of
SIREN SOUND

Smalltown is very small. Duh. I know.

But once it was a lot bigger. Tourists came and went, brought by ferries and sea planes and helicopters. For a brief moment, it appeared on the maps. And all because of the Sirens. The Sirens in the Sound.

You're probably too young to remember. Those were the Sirens that sang to the passengers on the ferries, and made national headlines. What a sensation they were! Photo-ops galore, with great debates over whether they were really sirens or just pods of sea otters.

The Reporter who broke the story became a national celebrity, and the woman who saw them first—Laura—the one who took off her clothes and dived from the ferry into the ocean, was inundated with admirers. So much so that she had to lock her doors, go out in disguise, and even then, they usually found her. She and the Reporter—weren't they a couple now? He was often by her side. Someone caught a photo of them kissing, though that may have been a doctored. Someone definitely caught them fighting, and fighting is what lovers do, isn't it?

At any rate, the Sirens messed it up. They started to sing again, and passengers on the ferries started to jump naked into the ocean in droves. Not many were found by Search and Rescue, maybe only one or two, and those tourists didn't remember anything, like they'd been hypnotized.

The news turned against the Sirens, and public opinion too. The Sirens were clearly monsters, preying on mankind. They must be destroyed! Call the Army! Or the Navy! Or both! But then, the environmentalists weighed in, pointing out that the Sirens were indigenous creatures and had rights too. It almost became a war.

Then, one day, it stopped.

Just completely stopped. It was the same day the Reporter disappeared and was never seen again. Some say they saw him on a ferry, naked, standing on a railing, but no one really saw him jump. They did find his backpack though. His wallet had a picture of Laura, the woman who first saw the Sirens, but she said she didn't know anything about it. In fact, she confessed to lying about the Sirens, to cover up the fact that she had an incurable disease and was just

trying to die on her own terms in the ocean. So that was the end of that.

Then, somehow it was years later.

I don't know why Laura agreed to see me. It wasn't like we had actually been in love. Or had we? Maybe we could have been, or maybe she answered the door because she felt sorry for me. Maybe it was the barnacles on my face. It was late and dark, and we drank coffee and caught up. She told me about her miraculous cure from that life-threatening disease, for which she thanked the Sirens. She'd managed to start her life again, said she'd always wanted to be a Librarian, it was always so quiet there. I told her about the place under the sea, and the battle with the octopuses, and the dead tourists I had for friends. I tried to tell her how beautiful it was, surrounded by the Sirens and their songs and gentle caresses, but it just sounded creepy so we hugged and said goodbye and I never saw her again.

I do think about her though, and what might have been. But I never went back. I don't think I'm much to look at now, and I smell like fish, and I can tell it's not her cup of tea.

As for Smalltown, it sank out of sight and out of mind and disappeared from the maps again. Good thing too. You don't want to ruin a good thing by letting it get out of control, do you? Even a Siren song will end someday.

Or will it? It hasn't yet, but I'll let you know.

The tale of
THE HOUSE ON ENDLESS STREET

He's running fast, the Boy with the wolf eyes. He's running to me.

All right, he's not really a boy. Not a human boy, at any rate. He's one of the sidhe, or whatever they are called.

All I know is he took me to my lost Mother, when the others would have abandoned me. And he gave me my first kiss. None of the other kisses I've known count. Those were kisses goodnight or hello, no more than handshakes. The Boy's kiss was daring, rude, invading, sweet. It sent my head spinning. I wanted to run away and towards him both. He only kissed me once, but every time I see his lips and his feral teeth, I see the second one waiting.

Mother calls me from the other direction. She holds the door open, the door to freedom. She is emaciated, her eyes large and luminous. She pleads with me. Close the door. Close it before he gets here. "He" is the Boy I have kissed, and "he" is also her former captor. Or is he? Wasn't that the House? How can a House capture anything? Surely I made that up. The Boy says I did. Mother says otherwise. Who to believe? I have to choose quickly. He will be here in moments.

Behind the Boy, there is a huge tidal wave. It surges across the ballroom. The Boy can outrun it, but not if I shut the door. Mother says I must do that. She says it urgently.

I try to clear my head. Once upon a time…that's how to begin, is it not? Once upon a time my Mother inherited this house, the House on Endless Street. Far across the water from our farm—the farm we knew and the farm we loved. The House was in a town of strangers. A giant house, fit for a Queen. Mother's Great Aunt Evelyn lived here, left it to her in her will. I never met Great Aunt Evelyn, but her picture hung above the giant fireplace in the dining hall downstairs. She looked like an old tree. Upright. Unbreakable. But her eyes twinkled in the portrait, and followed you around the room, and I thought she looked kind. I'm sure he didn't leave the House to Mother to curse her.

But curse her it did. One day, Mother disappeared, leaving a note that said she'd run off, back across the sea with another man. It was a lie—it wasn't even her handwriting—but Father believed it anyway. He went after her, leaving me in the House with a caretaker who never came back after the first day.

But about the Boy.

The Boy showed up the next day. He was with the elves, or the sidhe, and they were sneaking into my room, creeping towards my bed. I threw on the light and shrieked, which made them shriek too. Everyone shrieked but the Boy. He simply bowed to me, but I think now it was to hide his wolf smile. He was never afraid of anything, the Boy. Not even now, running before a tidal wave that is ripping the gilded portraits from the wall, and the walls themselves beginning to crumble. His eyes never leave mine. I find I can't look away either. Mother tries to run to help me close the door, but the floorboards warp into claws that hold her back. It really is alive, this House. I remember now.

The House is alive and it steals things. It can't help it, that's just how it is. It had stolen a subterranean kingdom from the elves, who had come to get it back. And it had stolen my Mother too. I insisted on going along. The elves said no, but the Boy said yes, and the Boy won. The Boy always won.

He opened a secret door in the floorboards under my bed, and we went down. Down past the basement, down a long stone spiral of stairs, staying close to their pale lanterns. Down into darkness and strange smells. Moisture made my nightgown cling, my hair wet.

Eventually, we got in a small boat and set sail for a distant light. As the light grew, I realized we were sailing across a room so vast you couldn't see the walls on the other side. It was like that everywhere—rooms that had grown to hide stolen things: oceans, castles, prehistoric monsters. There were chambers crammed with stolen art, from paintings to colossal statues. One held a sphynx and a pyramid, as well as a desert. The Boy explained: the house was a kleptomaniac. It compulsively stole things and built room after room, deeper and deeper into the Earth, to hide them in. It steals people too, he said then, and when I said "Mother," he raised his long eyebrows as if to say "Why not?". I found myself on the edge of tears then. He put an arm around me and said "Don't worry, we'll find her." He pulled away then, but kept hold of my hand. Just as he holds my eyes now, running for the door.

So many emotions surround me, my own tsunami, trying to drown me. I can barely hear my Mother's cries. The Boy reaches out for the door handle. I start to reach back for him. Then, incredibly, he stumbles.

I am no longer looking into his eyes. And I remember…

We reach the heart of the House. There we find, not Mother, but Great Aunt Evelyn. She is tied to a machine, valves and dials and strange lung-like bellows surround her. She is dry as a locust now, her skin waxy brown, the life almost sucked out of her. There is no twinkle in her eyes now., as they drift across my face without recognition. I scream. I scream until there are no more screams left and still try to make the sound. The elves have grabbed me now, and are dragging me away to a prison cage. The Boy watches, but for once, he doesn't smile.

Mother was in the cage next to mine. She rushed to me, her fingers touching my face. through the bars. No one needed to explain anything. It was clear the House could not survive on its own. It needed something from the living, something it extracted until all that was left was skin and bone. Then it tossed the husk aside, and reached for the next one.

And the Boy? Clearly a servant of the House. The Elven Kingdom was a ruse. They had been coming for me all along. And I had let them take me. I did it for my Mother, even when I knew something was wrong. I didn't listen to myself. And the one time I did…

The Boy was getting to his feet now, just as the spray of the giant wave showered around him. As he raised his face to mine, I remember seeing it through the bars as he freed me from my prison. When the door opened, he kissed me. He kissed me and time stopped. I forgot everything except his lips and his eyes. For a moment, there was something I had not seen there before. I'm still can't name it. I don't want to name it.

My Mother broke the spell. I'm sure rescuing her was not the original plan, but the Boy let her out and bowed. When he rose, my Mother slapped him.

I was stunned, then found myself between them, defending the Boy. What a strange thing. Here we were, in the midst of an escape, arguing and going nowhere fast. No wonder they almost caught us.

It was the House that saved the day.

The elves poured into the prison and surrounded us. The Boy pulled his knife and began to fight. Then, clear as day, I heard a frail old voice in my mind. "Run, child," it said. "Run. I cannot control the House for long." Behind us, a gap opened in the wall. I grabbed Mother's hand and bolted for the opening. When I saw it led up out of the darkness, I stopped. "Wait!" I said. "We have to go back—" "It's too late for me, child," the voice whispered. "Go…before it is too late."

I'd like to say I didn't listen. That we went back and freed Great Aunt Evelyn, destroyed the machines. We didn't though. We ran.

I have no right to judge.

So about the Boy…

I remember back on the farm, before we moved to the House on Endless Street. There had been a bird, a pigeon, that had been savaged by a cat. The feathers and most of the skin and muscles of its neck were missing. I ran and got my father. He picked up a shovel, and when he saw the bird he told me to turn my back. I didn't, so I saw him bring the shovel down quickly on the bird, squashing it flat. When he saw that I had been watching, he knelt down and took me by the shoulders. "Sometimes, when something has been so badly damaged, it is kindest to let it go."

The Boy was on his feet again. His eyes locked onto mine, and I felt the kiss again on my lips. I have no right to judge. I do it anyway.

I slammed the door in his face. And locked it.

It's been many years since then. The House on Endless Street is no more, collapsed into a pit so deep it seemed to go to the center of the Earth.

Mother and Father are long gone too, though they found each other again and had many happy years.

As for me, I am now as old as Great Aunt Evelyn. I do not kiss, not even to say hello. Sometimes, it is kindest to let it go.

The tale of
THE FIRST WAR OF THE WORLDS
(Anachronistically translated from various Martian spirit-messages)

Message One

Dear Pod,

May the Eternal One light your way.

Week one, here on Blue. I found my Tripod crew already stomping about, shooting their heat-rays at each other, crazy for action. I confess, I was even more crazed than they were.

At last, I gave the command. "Martians! Exterminate!" And off we went.

We waded along the jungle shores, hunting pests. Of course we are still stuck with the shallows. Deeper water would be infinitely nicer, but the Ganamedians are touchy about those spawning grounds, and who in their right mind wants to start an interplanetary war?

Much has changed since you and I last spawned here. Blue is still uncomfortably hot and moist, and as usual, the extra gravity wilts your tentacles. But the pests all seem to have accessorized, with armor and spikes and horns and frills and studded club-tails, and many have grown to gargantuan size—many times larger than our tripods. One of them—a king of the carnivores—has a bite that can tear right through Martian metal, and yet such tiny arms that it can't even scratch its back. Bizarre!

As usual, I have taken to naming these new pests. I call the monsters with the tiny arms flap-mouths, for their giant, screaming jaws.

Fortunately, the flap-mouths are relatively easy to exterminate—our heat-rays cut through their hollow bones like blood-butter. Of course, I'm trying to stay on budget, and one doesn't want to overuse costly weaponry, especially with the spawning deadline our client has given me. Why the zombies in the Eternal City always leave pest control to the last minute is beyond me.

But there are many ways to skin a pest, and the flap-mouths are only moderately bright. It's easy enough to dig a simple pit and entice them to fall in, then quickly put them out of their misery. In fact, we have dispatched entire nests of them this way. With any luck, I shall be home in time for our Mooniversary (but no promises).

Fondly,

M.

Message Two

Dear Pod,

May the Eternal One shine on you always.

Did I say this would be easy? Well, let me suck the blood out of those words!

Everything was going just fine. The local pests seemed to be subdued, and the Crabs have arrived and started digging the nest. I even got a note of congratulations from the Eternal City! No payment yet, of course, not even the first installment, but that's bureaucracy for you.

So here I was getting ready to wrap things up, when a well-organized squadron of flap-mouths—yes, I said squadron—ambushed and destroyed two of my tripods!

It happened again this morning, though I was able to rescue one this time (the repair crew is doing their best to make it functional, even though its heat-ray has been bitten off).

Of course, the beastly climate and gravity are not doing us any favors. By now, everyone is exhausted and ready to go home. Needless to say, no one has been paid yet either, ouch for morale.

All of which to say, don't wait for me for our Mooniversary celebrations. I have faced cunning pests before but rarely one that has taken such a sudden leap in intelligence. I must get to the bottom of this—and fast—before things get out of control!

In haste,

M.

Message Three

Dearest Pod,

May the Eternal One brighten your days.

It has become all-out war with the flap-mouths now, an absolute fustercluck. Their terrifying leader, whom I have named Frightwood, has even managed to enlist the other pests to its cause now, including the giant plant-eaters! Squadrons of flap-mouths cause the others to stampede and decimate the perimeter, no matter what their casualties. It seems everyone is more afraid of Frightwood than they are of our heat-rays. Unbelievable!

This leader of theirs seems peculiarly bright and strategic. It seems, if I may blaspheme, almost Martian! I shall take matters into my own tentacles and pour my resources into hunting it down today. It is, of course, no real match for me, but I confess, I look forward to our duel!

Anon,

M.

Message Four

My dear Pod,

May the Eternal One brighten our darkest days.

The universe has gone mad! Some little snitch has reported me, claiming I was deliberately sabotaging our mission to secure the spawning grounds, and without so much as a hello, the Eternal City have ordered a mighty stonk—an asteroid air strike!

Are they insane? This will spoil the spawning grounds on Blue for generations, for Martians and Ganamedians alike! It's almost like some idiot is trying to start a war! I'll bet it's our new Jeddor. Remember his slogan? If you can't beat them, use a bigger stick. May the Eternal One save us!

I am told the Green Comet teamsters have already sent one of their Planet-Busters hurtling towards us. We must leave *today* or suffer the consequences.

The Mechanics and the Crabs have already departed, but I tell you now, my dear Pod, with heavy hearts, I cannot go with them. Frightwood has made this a battle of honor, and I must exterminate him ere I go.

I confess this monster has outwitted me at every turn. I swear it is possessed of a greater cunning than any pest I have ever known. Even the Skin-flayers of the Great Canals were a walk in the red sands compared to Frightwood. If I give up now, I would die of shame or worse, become such a wretched thing that even you would despise me. This way, even if I fail, my nemesis and I shall both perish in the impact of the Planet-Buster, and you shall get the death bonus.

Forever yours,

M.

Message Five

My one and only Pod,

I send this message via the Eternal One, the great Illuminator.

Today, the most incredible thing has happened.

My second-to-last encounter with Frightwood was a disaster. I was out-Martianed, out-witted, and out of luck. Suffice it to say, I escaped, temporarily, in a smashed and barely functional tripod, my heat-ray hanging by a thread, and waited for a final, and likely fatal, showdown with my deadly enemy.

And as I waited, I heard a strange voice in my head. I'm pretty sure it was not one of the Ancestors. It was not even a Martian voice, yet I understood what it was saying.

The voice, at first, sounded confused, even afraid. It clearly didn't know where it was, for it didn't recognize any of the sights it could see through my eyes. To my surprise, I found a familiar pattern in its way of thinking and—color me crazy—I believe it was some kind of pest. It acted as if two arms and two legs were the norm, not tentacles, and the beating of two hearts an oddity. It reminded me of certain small creatures I discovered here, furry scavengers, greatly flawed but full of promise as domestic pets. How this pest came to inhabit my mind, I have no clue, but there it was, and at least it was somewhat friendly.

I had nothing else to do but await a bloody death from Frightwood or the Planet-Buster, so I engaged it in conversation. In fact, I told it everything.

The mind-spirit was a good listener, and talking to it felt as good as a blood snack. I fact, I found myself perking up, even in my desperate state. In gratitude, I named it Po, after you, dear Pod.

Which, as fate would have it, is when my nemesis showed up.

Of course, now the asteroid was visible in the sky and impact was immanent; soon we would both be fertilizing the countryside. But—wonder of wonders, just as Frightwood landed on my tripod and brought us crashing to the mud, yes, even as it ripped the metal roof from the cockpit and dragged me outside by my tentacles, the mind-spirit Po emitted from my lips a shocking noise—a kind of happy whooping sound—that so completely charmed my enemy that it immediately stopped snarling and became…friendly.

Too late for all of us, of course, as the comet races towards Blue and the air begins to burn. But oh! what joy to see my nemesis finally overcome, and from a sound that emanated from MY lips!

So goodbye, my Pod. May sanity prevail and let you live to find other tentacles to spawn with, but pray do not forget mine. I send you this spirit-message now as I fix my eyes upon the Eternal One, shining through the smoke-blackened sky like a bright red light.

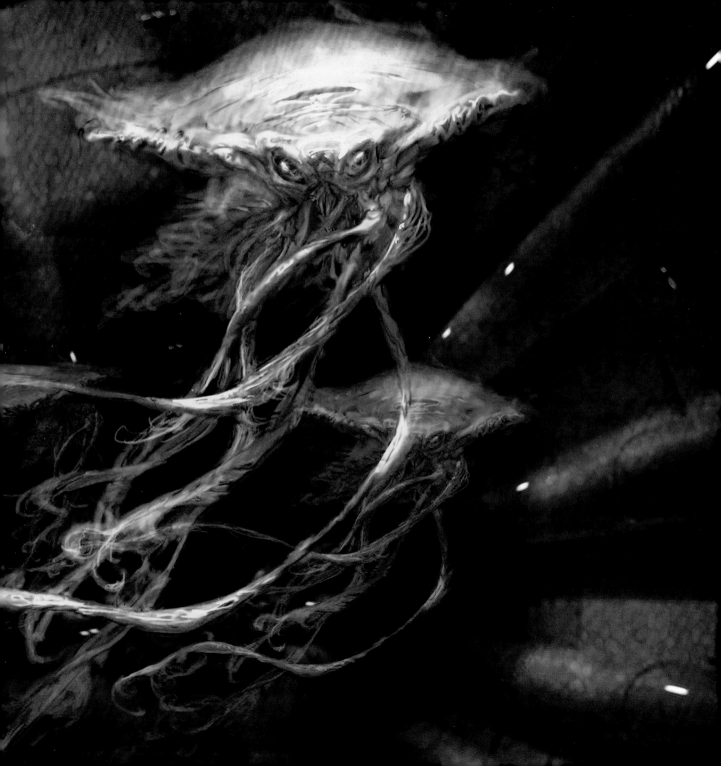

The tale of
THE TWO GHOSTS – Part Two

The Aliens shuttled back to their ships and departed as quickly as they came. I found myself alone on the Smalltown asteroid with the Two Ghosts.

"Thank you," I said. "I'm—"

"We know who you are." Frightwood bared his blue teeth.

"No…I meant to say, I'm sorry I left you here so long."

"Aw, he's just being friendly," said Po. "And you're welcome. As for that other thing, forget about it. You came back, didn't ya?"

Frightwood leaned towards Po, his lanky hair hiding his face. Po bobbed his Halloween apple head. "Before you go, we have one more story, just for you."

Frightwood leered at me. "Tell anyone and I will hunt you down and haunt you forever."

"And when you do tell them," said Po, "tell them not to tell anybody either, okay?"

I crossed my fingers behind my back and said, "Okay." So here's their last story, just for you.

The tale of
THE TWO BOYS

The boy with the red hair sat up in bed, scribbling furiously in a fat sketchbook. He was alone, here in the dark of a basement, except for a circle of lamplight pressing back the shadows. A Ray Bradbury book lay open beside him, filling his nostrils with the heady scent of second-hand bookstores. His 4B pencil smeared a little as he drew a Tyrannosaurus Rex munching on a bunch of big game hunters.

A sharp tap on the basement window, and he looked up, blinking. He saw the face of another boy, hair black as sin, pressed against the dusty glass. "Psst!" the face said. "Hey! Open up!"

Edgar slid the window open, careful not to let it squeak. It squeaked anyway. "What the hell, Bram? My Dad's going to kill me. It's the middle of the night!"

"Never mind that. I've got something to show you. Come on!"

Edgar looked nervously at the stairs. His Dad was a bodybuilder. He wouldn't kill his own son, but he might put his head through the ceiling. "If Dad finds out—"

"Keep talking, dumbo, and he might."

Moments later, they were stampeding through the sleeping town, their runners slapping pavement all the way to the sign that pointed twenty different directions, like it was the hub of the universe.

Bram doesn't have to tell Edgar where they're going. A quick climb over the wooden fence and a spit in the Wishing Well for good luck, and they touched down on the park bench underneath the old oak tree.

Edgar listened to a chorus of cicadas, male bugs, hoping to get lucky. "Well, what's the big revelation?" Edgar said.

"Time travel."

"Time what?"

"Time travel. Tonight I am going to teach you how to travel through time."

"Of course you are."

"I've been doing it for a while now," Bram's eyes squinched with wickedness. "I reckon you might be brave enough to try it too."

"Wait. You've been time traveling for real? Don't you know how dangerous that is? You change one little thing—"

"—and you could change the whole future! I know. I read Ray Bradbury too. But that can't happen the way I do it. We're just going to sit inside someone else head, somewhere else in time, and have a look around. You'll see!"

Edgar knew he'd follow Bram to Hell itself if he thought it was a good idea. And Mom always told him he shouldn't spend so much time in his own head. At least this way, he'd be in someone else's. "Okay," he said, "How do I do it?"

"Look up." Bram lifted his head, his dark eyes sparkling with starlight.

"See that red star there. That's not actually a star. That's the planet Mars."

"I know," said Edgar.

"Well, stare at it, Stare at it so hard that everything else goes black and vanishes."

Edgar stared. If Bram was pulling his leg, he was going to kill him. But after a long while, everything really did go black and vanish. Everything except the red star.

Edgar reached over and grabbed Bram's shoulder. "What are you doing?" Bram said.

"In case we get separated," the red-headed boy answered.

His black-haired friend laughed. "Ain't nothing ever gonna separate us, ol' Buddy."

But Edgar held tight anyway. He knew that strange things could happen, here in Smalltown.

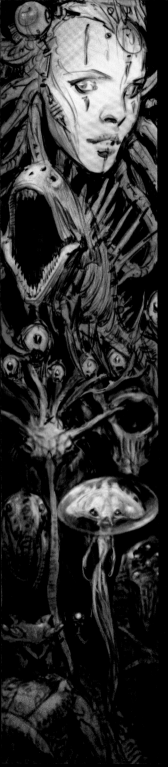

ACKNOWLEDGEMENTS

The Smalltown Tales are all true. Not non-fiction true, but true to the spirit of the amazing people I've met in my life. My heartfelt gratitude for our encounters and the indelible memories. These stories are proof that I have never forgotten you.

Great collaborators are worth more than their weight in gold, and I count my lucky stars to have had some of the best on this book. My thanks to Rachel Meinerding and Nicole Hendrix of the Concept Art Association, my guardian angels and Smalltown agents, and to Sian Parkhouse, editor extraordinaire, and her talented team at TITAN Books. I've always dreamt of working with TITAN; thank you for making reality outshine the dream.

Warm thanks to my Entertainment Attorneys, Diane Golden, and Sarah Lerner, for their wise counsel and legal wisdom. Likewise to my smarter older brother, Malcolm, for your timely astronomical insights, and to Mish Twombly, for your feedback and spider-walking assistance. My love and gratitude to my son and fellow story-lover, Inigo, and to my wife and muse, Leonor, for more than words or pictures can ever say.

Endless gratitude to the great Ray Bradbury, for implanting a love of words and dinosaurs that has lasted a lifetime. And to Mishi McCaig— my best reader, art director, and, lucky me, my daughter. This book only made it across the finish line because you ran beside me.

Finally, to Colin McCaig, who sits beside me on that park bench until the end of time. This book is for you, ol' buddy.

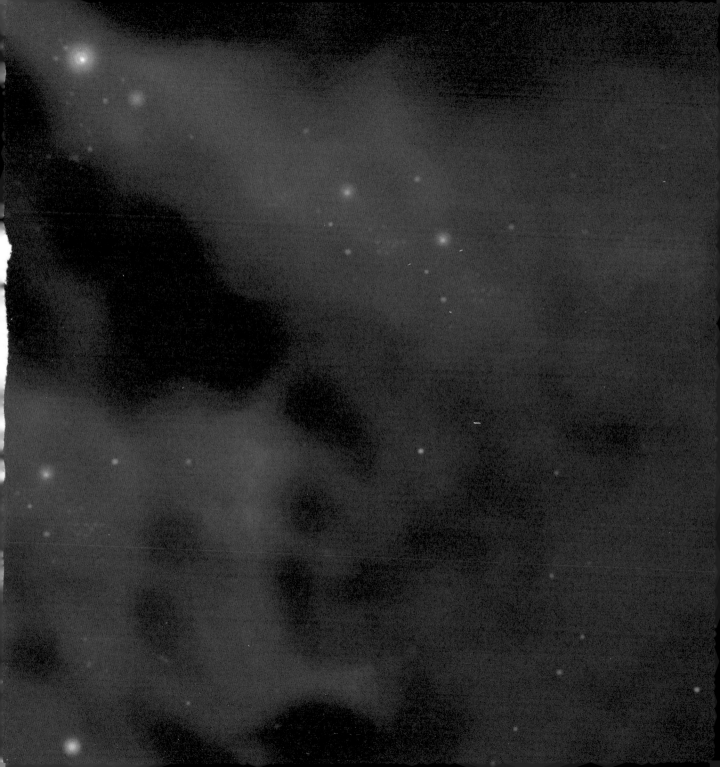